D0325946

STERLING CHILDREN'S BOOKS
New York

An Imprint of Sterling Publishing
387 Park Avenue South
New York, NY 10016

STERLING CHILDREN'S BOOKS and the distinctive Sterling Children's Books
logo are trademarks of Sterling Publishing Co., Inc.

© 2014 by Sterling Publishing Co., Inc.
Design by Jennifer Browning

All rights reserved. No part of this publication may be reproduced, stored in a
retrieval system, or transmitted in any form or by any means (including electronic,
mechanical, photocopying, recording, or otherwise) without prior written
permission from the publisher.

ISBN 978-1-4027-8428-6

Distributed in Canada by Sterling Publishing
c/o Canadian Manda Group, 165 Dufferin Street
Toronto, Ontario, Canada M6K 3H6
Distributed in the United Kingdom by GMC Distribution Services
Castle Place, 166 High Street, Lewes, East Sussex, England BN7 1XU
Distributed in Australia by Capricorn Link (Australia) Pty. Ltd.
P.O. Box 704, Windsor, NSW 2756, Australia

For information about custom editions, special sales, and premium and corporate
purchases, please contact Sterling Special Sales at 800-805-5489
or specialsales@sterlingpublishing.com.

Printed in China

Lot #:
2 4 6 8 10 9 7 5 3
03/17

www.sterlingpublishing.com/kids

SILVER PENNY STORIES

The Emperor's New Clothes

Told by Diane Namm

Illustrated by Ashley Mims

Once upon a time there was a foolish emperor. He loved to wear fancy clothes. Even more than wearing fancy clothes, he loved showing them off to everyone in his kingdom.

One day, two tricksters pretending to be tailors visited the emperor. They offered to sew a royal suit for him, made of the finest cloth.

"Your Highness," the tailors whispered loudly in the emperor's ear. "This cloth is so fine that it looks invisible to anyone who is foolish. A fool cannot see it!"

"We will weave this fine cloth from gold thread and make a suit especially for you. There will be nothing like it in all the land," the tricksters promised the emperor.

"Perfect!" the emperor said. "I will have a new suit *and* a way to find out who the fools in my kingdom are." He paid the tricksters two bags of gold coins to begin.

The two tricksters asked for a grand chamber and a loom to weave the cloth. They asked for delicate gold thread.

The tricksters pretended to cut, loom, and sew for days. The emperor's servants tiptoed in with food, drink, and whatever the tricksters wanted, whenever they called for it.

The emperor was very curious which of his subjects were secretly foolish. So he ordered his oldest and wisest advisor to check on the progress of the suit.

"We have woven almost all the cloth we will need," the tricksters assured the emperor's advisor. "Do you see how it glitters in the light? This fabric is the finest we've ever made."

The advisor saw nothing.

Am I foolish? he asked himself.

The advisor did not want the tricksters to know he saw nothing.

He went back to report to the emperor.

"Your Highness, the cloth is magnificent. Yours will surely be the most beautiful suit in the land," the advisor lied.

Excited, the emperor commanded the tailors bring the cloth at once for him to see.

The two tricksters pretended to
carry a large, heavy roll of fabric.

"Your Highness, the cloth is done.
Now we must measure you for your
suit," they said.

The emperor saw nothing at all.

Am I foolish? he worried.

He did not want the tricksters to think he saw nothing. So he, too, pretended the cloth was the most wonderful fabric he'd ever seen.

The two tricksters measured the emperor from head to toe. They cut and clipped through the air with their scissors. They sewed busily with needles to make a suit of invisible cloth. They worked eagerly to complete all the finishing touches.

"We are done!" exclaimed
the tricksters.

The emperor took off his old clothes.
The tricksters draped the new suit on
him and brought him to the mirror.

"Do you like it?" they asked.

The emperor turned bright red.
He saw no suit at all! But he did
not want to admit it.

"Magnificent! The style is so elegant.
The fabric is so light!" he lied.

"You must show it off to the rest of
your kingdom," the tricksters said.

The emperor planned a grand parade through his kingdom to show off his new suit. All his subjects gathered in the main square. Everyone wanted to see the emperor's wonderful new clothes.

Atop his royal carriage, the emperor rode proudly through the crowd. Everyone gazed at him in astonishment. The emperor was not wearing any clothes!

Am I a fool? they each wondered.

Nobody wanted to admit they saw nothing. They all believed everyone else could see the emperor's new clothes, so they all pretended, as well.

"Beautiful!" called one.

"Wonderful suit!" proclaimed another.

"What colors!" shouted a third.

"Marvelous!" said the others.

The emperor smiled proudly.

The tricksters clapped their hands with glee. They twirled and danced around each other. The crowd's reaction was exactly what they wanted.

But then a young boy pushed through the crowd.

"The emperor has no clothes on!" he called out.

The subjects stopped cheering, and for a moment the crowd was silent. Then his subjects started laughing!

The emperor knew the boy was right, but he continued his parade anyway. He ignored the laughing and whispers from the crowd. He pretended that everyone else in his kingdom was a fool.

But the tricksters knew the truth was discovered! They ran away quickly and were never heard from again.